The Moon Ribbon
and Other Tales

The Moon Ribbon

and Other Tales

by Jane Yolen

illustrated by
David Palladini

Thomas Y. Crowell Company
New York

Other books by Jane Yolen

THE BIRD OF TIME
THE GIRL WHO LOVED THE WIND
THE WIZARD ISLANDS
THE BOY WHO HAD WINGS
THE GIRL WHO CRIED FLOWERS AND OTHER TALES
RAINBOW RIDER
THE MAGIC THREE OF SOLATIA
THE TRANSFIGURED HART

Library of Congress Cataloging in Publication Data
Yolen, Jane H. The moon ribbon, and other tales.
SUMMARY: Six fairy tales: The Moon Ribbon, The Honey-
Stick Boy, Rosechild, Sans Soleil, Somewhen, and The Moon
Child. 1. Fairy tales. [1. Fairy tales] I. Palladini, David.
II. Title.   PZ8.Y78Mo   [Fic]   75-34462
ISBN 0-690-01044-3

1   2   3   4   5   6   7   8   9   10

Contents

For: Dale, Nancy,
Shulamith and Monday Eve

The Moon Ribbon
and Other Tales

The Moon Ribbon

There was once a plain but goodhearted girl named Sylva whose sole possession was a ribbon her mother had left her. It was a strange ribbon, the color of moonlight, for it had been woven from the gray hairs of her mother and her mother's mother and her mother's mother's mother before her.

Sylva lived with her widowed father in a great house by the forest's edge. Once the great house had belonged to her mother, but when she died, it became Sylva's father's house to do with as he willed. And what he willed was to live simply and happily with his daughter without thinking of the day to come.

But one day, when there was little enough to live on, and only the great house to recommend him, Sylva's father married again, a beautiful widow who had two beautiful daughters of her own.

It was a disastrous choice, for no sooner were they wed when it was apparent the woman was mean in spirit and meaner in tongue. She dismissed most of

1

the servants and gave their chores over to Sylva, who followed her orders without complaint. For simply living in her mother's house with her loving father seemed enough for the girl.

After a bit, however, the old man died in order to have some peace, and the house passed on to the stepmother. Scarcely two days had passed, or maybe three, when the stepmother left off mourning the old man and turned on Sylva. She dismissed the last of the servants without their pay.

"Girl," she called out, for she never used Sylva's name, "you will sleep in the kitchen and do the charring." And from that time on it was so.

Sylva swept the floor and washed and mended the family's clothing. She sowed and hoed and tended the fields. She ground the wheat and kneaded the bread, and she waited on the others as though she were a servant. But she did not complain.

Yet late at night, when the stepmother and her own two daughters were asleep, Sylva would weep bitterly into her pillow, which was nothing more than an old broom laid in front of the hearth.

One day, when she was cleaning out an old desk, Sylva came upon a hidden drawer she had never seen before. Trembling, she opened the drawer. It was empty except for a silver ribbon with a label attached to it. *For Sylva* read the card. *The Moon Ribbon of Her Mother's Hair.* She took it out and stared at it. And all that she had lost was borne in upon her. She felt the tears start in her eyes, and so as not to cry she took the tag off and began to stroke the ribbon with her hand. It was rough and smooth at once and shone like the rays of the moon.

At that moment her stepsisters came into the room.

"What is that?" asked one. "Is it nice? It is mine."

"I want it. I saw it first," cried the other.

The noise brought the stepmother to them. "Show it to me," she said.

Obediently, Sylva came over and held the ribbon out to her. But when the stepmother picked it up, it looked like no more than strands of gray hair woven together unevenly. It was prickly to the touch.

"Disgusting," said the stepmother dropping it back into Sylva's hand. "Throw it out at once."

"Burn it," cried one stepsister.

"Bury it," cried the other.

"Oh, please. It was my mother's. She left it for me. Please let me keep it," begged Sylva.

The stepmother looked again at the gray strand. "Very well," she said with a grim smile. "It suits you." And she strode out of the room, her daughters behind her.

Now that she had the silver ribbon, Sylva thought her life would be better. But instead it became worse. As if to punish her for speaking out for the ribbon, her sisters were at her to wait on them both day and night. And whereas before she had to sleep by the hearth, she now had to sleep outside with the animals. Yet she did not complain or run away, for she was tied by her memories to her mother's house.

One night, when the frost was on the grass turning each blade into a silver spear, Sylva threw herself to the ground in tears. And the silver ribbon, which she had tied loosely about her hair, slipped off and lay on the ground before her. She had never seen it in the moonlight. It glittered and shone and seemed to ripple.

Sylva bent over to touch it and her tears fell upon it. Suddenly the ribbon began to grow and change, and as it changed the air was filled with a woman's soft voice speaking these words:

> *"Silver ribbon, silver hair,*
> *Carry Sylva with great care,*
> *Bring my daughter home."*

And there at Sylva's feet was a silver river that glittered and shone and rippled in the moonlight.

There was neither boat nor bridge, but Sylva did not care. She thought the river would wash away her sorrows, and without a single word, she threw herself in.

But she did not sink. Instead she floated like a

swan and the river bore her on, on past houses and hills, past high places and low. And strange to say, she was not wet at all.

At last she was carried around a great bend in the river and deposited gently on a grassy slope that came right down to the water's edge. Sylva scrambled up onto the bank and looked about. There was a great meadow of grass so green and still it might have been painted on. At the meadow's rim, near a dark forest, sat a house that was like and yet not like the one in which Sylva lived.

"Surely someone will be there who can tell me where I am and why I have been brought here," she thought. So she made her way across the meadow and only where she stepped down did the grass move. When she moved beyond, the grass sprang back and was the same as before. And though she passed lark-spur and meadowsweet, clover and rye, they did not seem like real flowers, for they had no smell at all.

"Am I dreaming?" she wondered, "or am I dead?" But she did not say it out loud, for she was afraid to speak into the silence.

Sylva walked up to the house and hesitated at the door. She feared to knock and yet feared equally not to. As she was deciding, the door opened of itself and she walked in.

She found herself in a large, long, dark hall with a single crystal door at the end that emitted a strange

glow the color of moonlight. As she walked down the hall, her shoes made no clatter on the polished wood floor. And when she reached the door, she tried to peer through into the room beyond, but the crystal panes merely gave back her own reflection twelve times.

Sylva reached for the doorknob and pulled sharply. The glowing crystal knob came off in her hand. She would have wept then, but anger stayed her; she beat her fist against the door and it suddenly gave way.

Inside was a small room lit only by a fireplace and a round white globe that hung from the ceiling like a pale, wan moon. Before the fireplace stood a tall woman dressed all in white. Her silver-white hair was unbound and cascaded to her knees. Around her neck was a silver ribbon.

"Welcome, my daughter," she said.

"Are you my mother?" asked Sylva wonderingly, for what little she remembered of her mother, she remembered no one as grand as this.

"I am if you make me so," came the reply.

"And how do I do that?" asked Sylva.

"Give me your hand."

As the woman spoke, she seemed to move away, yet she moved not at all. Instead the floor between them moved and cracked apart. Soon they were separated by a great chasm which was so black it seemed to have no bottom.

8

"I cannot reach," said Sylva.

"You must try," the woman replied.

So Sylva clutched the crystal knob to her breast and leaped, but it was too far. As she fell, she heard a woman's voice speaking from behind her and before her and all about her, warm with praise.

"Well done, my daughter. You are halfway home."

Sylva landed gently on the meadow grass, but a moment's walk from her house. In her hand she still held the knob, shrunk now to the size of a jewel. The river shimmered once before her and was gone, and where it had been was the silver ribbon, lying limp and damp in the morning frost.

The door to the house stood open. She drew a deep breath and went in.

"What is that?" cried one of the stepsisters when she saw the crystalline jewel in Sylva's hand.

"I want it," cried the other, grabbing it from her.

"I will take that," said the stepmother, snatching it from them all. She held it up to the light and examined it. "It will fetch a good price and repay me for my care of you. Where did you get it?" she asked Sylva.

Sylva tried to tell them of the ribbon and the river, the tall woman and the black crevasse. But they laughed at her and did not believe her. Yet they could not explain away the jewel. So they left her then and went off to the city to sell it. When they returned,

9

it was late. They thrust Sylva outside to sleep and went themselves to their comfortable beds to dream of their new riches.

Sylva sat on the cold ground and thought about what had happened. She reached up and took down the ribbon from her hair. She stroked it, and it felt smooth and soft and yet hard, too. Carefully she placed it on the ground.

In the moonlight, the ribbon glittered and shone. Sylva recalled the song she had heard, so she sang it to herself:

"Silver ribbon, silver hair,
Carry Sylva with great care,
Bring my daughter home."

Suddenly the ribbon began to grow and change, and there at her feet was a silver highway that glittered and glistened in the moonlight.

Without a moment's hesitation, Sylva got up and stepped out onto the road and waited for it to bring her to the magical house.

But the road did not move.

"Strange," she said to herself. "Why does it not carry me as the river did?"

Sylva stood on the road and waited a moment

more, then tentatively set one foot in front of the other. As soon as she had set off on her own, the road set off, too, and they moved together past fields and forests, faster and faster, till the scenery seemed to fly by and blur into a moon-bleached rainbow of yellows, grays, and black.

The road took a great turning and then quite suddenly stopped, but Sylva did not. She scrambled up the bank where the road ended and found herself again in the meadow. At the far rim of the grass, where the forest began, was the house she had seen before.

Sylva strode purposefully through the grass, and this time the meadow was filled with the song of birds, the meadowlark and the bunting and the sweet jug-jug-jug of the nightingale. She could smell fresh-mown hay and the pungent pine.

The door of the house stood wide open, so Sylva went right in. The long hall was no longer dark but filled with the strange moonglow. And when she reached the crystal door at the end, and gazed at her reflection twelve times in the glass, she saw her own face set with strange gray eyes and long gray hair. She put her hand up to her mouth to stop herself from crying out. But the sound came through, and the door opened of itself.

Inside was the tall woman all in white, and the globe above her was as bright as a harvest moon.

"Welcome, my sister," the woman said.

"I have no sister," said Sylva, "but the two step-sisters I left at home. And you are none of those."

"I am if you make me so."

"How do I do that?"

"Give me back my heart which you took from me yesterday."

"I did not take your heart. I took nothing but a crystal jewel."

The woman smiled. "It was my heart."

Sylva looked stricken. "But I cannot give it back. My stepmother took it from me."

"No one can take unless you give."

"I had no choice."

"There is always a choice," the woman said.

Sylva would have cried then, but a sudden thought struck her. "Then it must have been your choice to give me your heart."

The woman smiled again, nodded gently, and held out her hand.

Sylva placed her hand in the woman's and there glowed for a moment on the woman's breast a silvery jewel that melted and disappeared.

"Now will you give me your heart?"

"I have done that already," said Sylva, and as she said it, she knew it to be true.

The woman reached over and touched Sylva on her breast and her heart sprang out onto the woman's hand and turned into two fiery red jewels. "Once given, twice gained," said the woman. She handed one of the jewels back to Sylva. "Only take care that you give each jewel with love."

Sylva felt the jewel warm and glowing in her hand and at its touch felt such comfort as she had not in many days. She closed her eyes and a smile came on her face. And when she opened her eyes again, she was standing on the meadow grass not two steps from her own door. It was morning, and by her feet lay the silver ribbon, limp and damp from the frost.

The door to her house stood open.

Sylva drew in her breath, picked up the ribbon, and went in.

"What has happened to your hair?" asked one step-sister.

"What has happened to your eyes?" asked the other.

For indeed Sylva's hair and eyes had turned as silver as the moon.

But the stepmother saw only the fiery red jewel in Sylva's hand. "Give it to me," she said, pointing to the gem.

At first Sylva held out her hand, but then quickly drew it back. "I *can* not," she said.

The stepmother's eyes became hard. "Girl, give it here."

"I *will* not," said Sylva.

The stepmother's eyes narrowed. "Then you shall tell me where you got it."

"That I shall, and gladly," said Sylva. She told them of the silver ribbon and the silver road, of the house with the crystal door. But strange to say, she left out the woman and her words.

The stepmother closed her eyes and thought. At last she said, "Let me see this wondrous silver ribbon, that I may believe what you say."

Sylva handed her the ribbon, but she was not fooled by her stepmother's tone.

The moment the silver ribbon lay prickly and limp in the stepmother's hand, she looked up triumphantly at Sylva. Her face broke into a wolfish grin. "Fool," she said, "the magic is herein. With this ribbon there are jewels for the taking." She marched out of the door and the stepsisters hurried behind her.

Sylva walked after them, but slowly, stopping in the open door.

The stepmother flung the ribbon down. In the early morning sun it glowed as if with a cold flame.

"Say the words, girl," the stepmother commanded.

From the doorway Sylva whispered:

"Silver ribbon, silver hair,
Lead the ladies with great care,
Lead them to their home."

The silver ribbon wriggled and writhed in the sunlight, and as they watched, it turned into a silver-red stair that went down into the ground.

"Wait," called Sylva. "Do not go." But it was too late.

With a great shout, the stepmother gathered up her skirts and ran down the steps, her daughters fast behind her. And before Sylva could move, the ground had closed up after them and the meadow was as before.

On the grass lay the silver ribbon, limp and dull. Sylva went over and picked it up. As she did so, the jewel melted in her hand and she felt a burning in her breast. She put her hand up to it, and she felt her heart beating strongly beneath. Sylva smiled, put the silver ribbon in her pocket, and went back into her house.

After a time, Sylva's hair returned to its own color, except for seven silver strands, but her eyes never changed back. And when she was married and had a child of her own, Sylva plucked the silver strands from her own hair and wove them into the silver ribbon, which she kept in a wooden box. When Sylva's child was old enough to understand, the box with the ribbon was put into her safekeeping, and she has kept them for her own daughter to this very day.

The Honey-Stick Boy

Once in the middle of a honey forest there lived a man and woman. They wanted a child and had none, so they prayed to the spirit of the hive to give them a child. But through the years, though they wept and prayed, neither son nor daughter was ever sent them.

At last they grew old and bitter.

One day the old woman took three long sticks she had been saving for the cookfire and made a figure with them.

"If we had a child like that," she said, pointing to the stick figure, "even so would I be happy. But what is the good of praying to the spirit of the hive if it cannot grant us this one thing?"

"Old woman," cautioned her husband, "watch how your tongue wags. For the little honey bees are the ears of the forest. And I would not want the spirit of the hive to hear what you have said."

"May his honey become as bitter as I," said the old woman, turning from her man.

She looked at the stick figure and held it up. "See, I have made a child where the spirit of the hive has failed. Even thus shall I make my own happiness."

Then she went to a nearby hollow tree not far from their camp and thrust her arm into the honeybee's nest. She did not mind the buzzing and the stinging, and she brought a handful of honey home.

"The sticks shall make my new son strong," said the old woman. "The honey shall make him sweet." And she shaped the sticks and honey into the figure of a slim boy, patting the sticky stuff into place.

"Where is it said that a boy should be sweet?" asked the old man gruffly.

"All people should be sweet," she replied.

And to this he had no answer. Yet still he feared that they had angered the spirit of the hive and he worried about this long into the night.

In the morning, when the two old people awoke, they found the fire had been laid, the dirt floor swept, and the table set for two.

"Who could have done such a thing?" asked the old man, marveling.

"Our son, of course," said the old woman. "For like all good sons, he helps his parents."

"You are mad," the old man began. But at that

moment, the door swung open and a slim boy came through, his arms full of berries, flowers, and a jug of wild grape wine.

"Good morning, my parents," he said, with a smile so sweet and strong the old man knew at once who it was.

So they called him Mellis, for his honied disposition. He lived with them happily for many days, helping cook and gather food, watching for wild animals at night, and singing softly to send them to sleep. And in all things he was as a human son to them save for these two: He did not eat nor did he sleep.

But the spirit of the hive was angry. The old man and the old woman no longer prayed to him. It was Mellis who brought them berries and wine. It was Mellis who found them feathers and fur. And it was Mellis for whom they saved their praise.

"They no longer remember how many years I gave them life. They grow old and forgetful. They think that they exist by their own wits alone, making a manikin of honey and sticks. But they forget whose honey it was that made him sweet and whose sticks it was that made him strong. I shall have to help them remember."

So the spirit of the hive sent a drone to listen while the old man and his new son talked. For surely there would fall from their lips some way to make the old people remember.

The bee flew high and the bee flew low and the bee flew in through the window of the hut. It hovered out of sight while Mellis served the old man and his woman their food.

"Today," the old man said to the boy, "we shall go down to the river. There I will teach you how to fish. A man must teach his son all he knows, for we do not live on berries alone. The forest and the river are as one in this life."

"But I do not dare go to the river, my father," replied Mellis.

"What is this?" asked the old man. "A boy does not disobey his father."

"In all things I am yours," said the boy, "save this. For should I fall in the river, the honey that makes me sweet will be washed away. And the sticks that make me strong will float downstream and out of sight."

"What nonsense," said the old woman angrily, for she had forgotten how she had made the boy and believed that he was as human as they.

"You will do as I say," said the old man.

And so Mellis did, for his nature was so sweet he could not disobey.

The drone heard all that was said, and sped back

through the forest to the great hive. When it had danced out its message, the spirit of the hive nodded.

"You have done well," said the spirit. "For now I know how to make the old man and old woman remember." And the spirit flew on gauzy wings to the river's edge.

Mellis and the old man had just come down to the bank. The old man flung a vine net into the river, saying, "And thus, my son, goes the cast."

The vine net settled quietly in the stream. The little fish swam round and about it but they did not disturb the lines.

Then the spirit of the hive sent a small swarm of drones into the river. As they dropped into the water, they struggled in the waves. Down in the depth of the river a big black fish, looking for food, saw the movement and swam slowly to the top. It swam right into the waiting net. The fish felt the net close upon it and twisted and turned and pulled the net in many different ways.

The old man was not prepared for such a great fish. His hands were caught in the twisting and he was pulled into the river.

"Ae-i!" he cried out as he fell. "My son, my son, catch hold of my foot!"

Obediently, Mellis reached for the old man's foot and caught hold.

The old man kicked and the old man thrashed, and Mellis held tight to his foot. But with one final pull the old man pulled Mellis right into the river with a splash.

As the water swept over the boy, it tore his pants, his sandals, and his shirt and ripped them from his body. It washed and it washed at his flailing limbs till honey-sweet hair and flesh and all were washed away and nothing was left but three long sticks that bobbed up to the top of the river.

The old man reached out for the sticks and caught hold. The sticks kept his head above the waves and carried him safely to shore. He crept up on the bank and lay there gasping out his thanks. He called to the spirit of the hive and blessed it for bringing him out of the stream.

But the sticks did not hear the thanks nor care. Caught up in the current, they bobbed and danced and raced down the river and were soon lost to sight.

The old man stood up wearily, pushed his wet hair from his eyes, and went home.

"A brave son," he told his wife. "He gave his life to save me."

"Now once more we have no child," said the old woman sadly, but she did not say it bitterly. For she had her dear husband safe and she had her memories, and it was hard to say which she treasured more.

As for the sticks that had been Mellis, they eventually touched shore and rooted together and grew into a mighty tree. And long after the old man and the old woman had passed away, the honey from that tree was known throughout the forest as the strongest and the sweetest in the world.

Rosechild

There once lived an old woman who longed for a child, though she was neither widow nor wed.

One day when she was out in the woods gathering herbs, she heard a cry. She saw nothing nearby but a flowering bush, so she went over to that. There, nestled in the petals of a wild rose, was a tiny babe.

Quickly the old woman picked the child up between her forefinger and thumb, and, wrapping it in her linen kerchief, she brought it to her home. There she made it a cradle from a walnut and lined the shell with soft wool. Then she sat back and wondered how to make the child grow.

"If it were a real child," thought she, "I would feed it pieces of bread sopped in honey and milk till it was quite grown up. But as it is a Rosechild, goodness alone knows what I must do, for I do not."

At last she got up and went to her neighbor Farmer Brow. For surely if anyone would know about raising a child who was born in a flower, a farmer would.

25

So she knocked on his door, and when Brow threw it open, she called:

> *"Farmer Brow, answer me now,*
> *How shall my Rosechild grow?"*

Farmer Brow scratched his head up under his hat and said, "Turn its soil and water it well," for he thought she meant a flowering bush.

So the old woman went home and turned the child around in its cradle and sprinkled it with water from the well. Then she sat down and watched the child for a day. But the Rosechild did not grow.

At last the old woman got up and went to her other neighbor, Squire Bray. For surely if anyone would know how to raise a child born in a flower, a squire would. So she knocked on his door, and when Bray answered it she called:

> *"Squire Bray, tell me the way*
> *To make my Rosechild grow."*

Squire Bray struck his riding stick against his boot and said, "Feed it mash and turn it out to pasture," for he thought she was talking about a horse.

So the old woman went home and fed the Rosechild a meal of mash and put it out into the meadow. Then

26

she settled down on the grass beside it and watched for a day. But the Rosechild did not grow.

At last she got up and put the child back in its walnut cradle and went to see the village priest, Father Bree. For surely if anyone would know how to raise a child born in a flower, a priest would. So she knocked on the vestry door. And when Father Bree came to see who was there, she called:

*"Father Bree, tell to me
How shall my Rosechild grow?"*

Father Bree fingered his beads and said, "Place it on the Good Book and make a cross on its forehead," for he thought the old woman was beset by a devil.

So the old woman went home and set the Rosechild upon the Good Book and made the sign of the cross on its forehead. Then she settled down and watched the child for a day. But still the Rosechild did not grow.

However, there was no one left to ask. So the old woman threw her apron up over her head and cried out loud:

*"Oh me, oh my,
My Rosechild will die."*

Just then a small wee voice called out from the walnut shell, "Mama."

The old woman took her apron off her head and saw the Rosechild holding up its hands. She reached over and plucked it up between her forefinger and thumb and cradled it to her cheek. She felt her love flowing out to the tiny child. And she loved it so much, it began to grow and grow and grow till it was old enough and big enough to care for the little old woman. It fed her pieces of bread sopped in milk and honey and anything else she needed or wanted. And from that day on, the house was always filled with the lovely scent of roses.

Sans Soleil

There was once a prince called Sans Soleil, which is to say Sunless. It had been prophesied at his birth that he would grow so handsome his beauty would outshine the sun. That he might not be killed by the jealous star, he had to be kept in the dark, for it was said that he would die if ever a shaft of sunlight fell upon his brow.

So the very night he was born, his father, the king, had him carried away to a castle that was carved out of rock. And in that candlelit cave-castle, the young prince grew and flourished without ever seeing the sun.

Now by the time Sans Soleil was twenty years old, the story of his strange beauty and of the evil prediction had been told at every hearth and hall in the kingdom. And every maiden of marrying age had heard his tragic tale.

But one in particular, Viga, the daughter of a duke, did not believe what she heard.

31

"Surely," she said, tossing her raven-black hair from her face, "surely the king has hidden his son from the light because he is too monstrous to behold."

Her father shook his head. "Nay," he replied. "I have been to this cave-castle and have seen this prince. He is handsomer than the sun."

But still Viga did not believe what her father told her. "The sun cannot harm anyone," she said. "There is no sense in what you say." And she took herself to the king dressed in her finest gown of silver and gold.

"Sire," she said, "at court you have been taken in by lies. The sun is not harmful. It nourishes. It causes all things to grow. It will not kill the prince."

The king was touched by the girl's sincerity. He was moved by her beauty. He was awed by her strength of purpose, for it is no little thing to contradict a king. Still, he shook his head and said, "It was prophesied at his birth that he would die if ever a shaft of sunlight struck his brow."

"Old wives and young babes believe such tales. They should not frighten you, Sire. They do not frighten me," Viga replied.

"They do not frighten you because you are not the one who would die," said the king, and at these words all the courtiers smiled and nodded their heads and murmured to one another. "Still, I will give the matter more thought."

Viga gave a low curtsey. And as she rose, she said quietly, so that only the king could hear it, "It does seem strange that *sun* and *son* do sound the same." Then she smiled brightly and departed.

The king was true to his word and gave the matter more thought. And what he concluded was this: that his son and Viga should be wed. For he liked her courage and admired her beauty, and thought she would make his son a most suitable wife. So the king and the duke set the wedding date for a week from the following night.

When the night was deep and no spot of sun still lit the kingdom, a carriage with drawn curtains arrived at Viga's door. Out stepped the handsomest man she had ever seen. He was dressed all in red and gold, like the sun.

They were wed by candlelight, and their golden rings were carved with images of the sun. There was feasting and dancing till three. Then the two talked and kissed far into the night as befits a couple who are but newly wed.

But at the crowing of the village cocks announcing that the sun would soon rise, Sans Soleil stood up. "I must go. I cannot allow the sun to shine upon me."

"Do not leave me," Viga said. "Now that we are wed, I cannot bear to have you away from my sight. Do not be afraid of the sun. It will not harm you. Stay here with me."

"No, I am safe only in my cave. You are my wife, come and live in my cave-castle with me."

"Live in a cave?" said Viga. "Never."

So the prince tore himself from her grasp and ran out into the waiting golden carriage. With a crack of the whip, the horses were away before the sun could gain the sky.

However, Viga was a woman of strong will. So determined was she to prove to Sans Soleil that she was right and he would not be killed by the sun, she devised a plan. That very day she sent her maid-servants to buy up all the cockerels in the kingdom. Then she had her footmen bind the birds and throw them down into the duke's deepest dungeons, where it would always be dark as night.

But there was one rooster the servants could not buy, the pet of the potter's boy. The child cried so much at the thought of losing his bird, his father would not part with it.

"What is one cockerel out of so many?" the servants asked themselves. And so they neglected to tell their mistress of the last bird.

That evening again Sans Soleil's carriage came to Viga's door. As before the prince was dressed all in red and gold, like the sun, and the feathers on his cap stood out like golden rays. In his hand he carried a sunburst, a ruby brooch with beams like a star.

"This is my only sun," he said to Viga. "Now it is yours."

And they forgave one another for the harsh words of the morn. They touched and kissed as married couples do, far into the night.

At the coming of the dawn, far off in the village, the cockerel belonging to the potter's child began to crow.

"Is that a cockerel I hear?" asked Sans Soleil, sitting up.

"There is no cockerel," replied Viga sleepily, for she thought indeed there was none.

But again the rooster crowed out, and, hearing no answering call from his brothers, he sang out louder than before.

"I am sure I hear the warning of the sun's approach," said Sans Soleil.

"It is nothing but a servant's snore," Viga replied. "Stay quiet. Stay asleep. Stay with me."

But on the third crow, Sans Soleil leaped up. "I must go," he said. "I cannot allow the sun to shine upon me."

"Do not put your faith in such old wives' tales," cried Viga. "The sun cannot hurt you. Put your faith in me."

But it was too late. The prince was gone, running down into his golden carriage and away to his cave-castle before the sun could start up in the sky.

However, Viga was a woman of strong will and passion. She was determined not to lose her lover for a single day because of such a foolish tale. She was convinced that if the prince but forgot the sun, he would learn that it could do him no harm. So she decided to have the last rooster put in her father's dungeon.

But she did not trust her servants anymore. With her cloak wrapped about her and covering her face with a sleeve, Viga slipped out into the streets. By the potter's hut she saw the bird strutting and preening its feathers in the sun. Quickly she looked around, but there was no one in sight. She reached down, snatched up the cockerel, and hid it under her cloak. In the night of her garment the bird made no sound.

She was back in her own home before the potter's child could set up his wail. The cockerel she put with its brothers in the dark. Then she waited impatiently for the sun to set that she might see her lover again.

That evening, so great was his haste, Sans Soleil himself drove the golden carriage to the door. He leaped to the ground and in a graceful bound ran to the waiting girl.

They ate and touched and sang and danced and talked until the night was through. But there were no cockerels to crow and warn them of the dawn.

Suddenly the prince glanced out of the window. "It is becoming light," he cried. "I must leave. You know that I cannot allow the sun to shine on me."

"Love me. Trust me. Stay with me," said Viga, smoothing his hair with her strong hands.

But Sans Soleil glanced out of the window again. "Is that the sun? Tell me, for I have never seen it shine."

Viga smoothed his neck with her fingers. "Forget your foolish fears. The sun nourishes. It does not kill. Stay with me here and greet the dawn."

The prince was moved by her plea and by his love for her. But just as he was about to stay, fear, like an old habit, conquered him. He jumped up and blinked at the light. "I must go to my cave. Only there will I be safe," he cried. And before she could stop him, he tore from her grasp and sped out into the dawn.

Viga ran after him. "Do not be afraid," she called. Her long black hair streamed out behind her like the rays of a black star. "It is but a tale. A tale for children. *You* are the sun."

But the prince did not hear her. As he ran out into the courtyard, the sun rose in full brilliance over the wall. Sans Soleil had never seen anything so glorious before. He stood and stared at the burning star. The sunlight struck him full in the face. And with a single cry of pain or anger or regret, he fell down dead.

Viga saw him fall. She cried out, "Oh, Sans Soleil,

it was true. Who would have believed it? Now it is I who am sunless, for you were my sun."

She threw herself upon his still form, her breast against his, her cool white brow on the ashes of his, and wept.

The next year, in the courtyard where Sans Soleil had fallen, a single sunflower grew. But unlike others of its kind, it bloomed all year round and always turned its face away from the sun.

Viga had a belvedere built around it. There she spent her days, tending the flower, watering it, and turning its soil.

When visitors arrived at her father's house, she would tell them the story of her love for Sans Soleil. And the story always ended with this caution: "Sometimes," Viga would say, "what we believe is stronger than what is true."

Somewhen

Once, and it does not matter what the day, a young boy named Tom was traveling down a road to seek his fortune. The road was long, the sun was hot, and finally, where the road forked, the boy saw a tree.

"There," thought he, "I will rest a while and think about my fortune. For whether it is good or bad, it is certain that it lies ahead of me."

And so thinking, the boy made his way to the tree. Only, when he came to it, he found its shadow occupied by an old man who lay asleep. Being a good boy, Tom sat down in the sun quietly and waited for the old man to waken and share the cooling shade with him.

At last the old man opened his eyes and signaled with them for Tom to come closer. And if by then the sun was down and shadows lay all about, Tom did not complain, for he knew his fortune lay ahead while the old man's lay behind.

"I am seeking my fortune, old man," said Tom. "Can you point which way is best?"

The old man looked up the road and down. He looked east and he looked west. Then he shook his head. "My eyes are poor," he said to Tom. "Used to be I could see the wind."

"Well then, grandfather," continued Tom, "perhaps you have heard which way the wide world lies."

The old man put his head to one side and listened. Then he put his head to the other. Then he shook it. "My ears are poor, too," said he. "Used to be I could hear the grass."

Tom sat down and puzzled over this for a while. "Old father," he said at last, "do you know of a place I could go? A place to seek my fortune?"

"*Somewhen* is the best I can say," said the old man. Then he looked strangely at Tom and added, "Three's enough." He creaked to his feet, stretched, and disappeared behind the tree. Tom, being a good boy, did not follow. Instead he settled himself under the branches and slept until morning. When the sun rose slowly in the east, Tom rose, too. And he chose the fork in the road he hoped would lead him to *Somewhen.*

Tom traveled many days and did many deeds. He dug gold in the hills and dived for pearls in the sea. He climbed mountains and descended into caves. He slept hungry and he slept full. And he saw all

there was to see in the world, and a lot more, too. But still he searched for *Somewhen*.

At last, however, he met a lovely girl whose hair was brushed with sunlight and whose hands were meant to rock cradles. And so Tom put *Somewhen* aside, planted grass and grain, and grew a world around his house.

And if he thought about *Somewhen*, it was as if it had been a tale he read one time as a child. It never troubled his mind at all.

Only one day, when he had grown old and his grandchildren sat by his side at the hearth and asked about the wide world, Old Tom told them about his travels.

"Yes," he said, "I roamed the world when I was young. Searching for things—I do not remember what. Found some. Didn't find others. But what was important was that I traveled some when I was young."

And then he stopped, for a memory caught him. "I traveled *some when* I was young. *Somewhen.*" Was that what the old man had meant? In the seeking was the finding? But Old Tom did not say that out loud.

And a few days later, Old Tom was sitting under a tree when a young lad, dusted with the road's winding, stopped a bit.

"Old man," said the lad, "I am seeking my fortune. Can you tell me which way to go?"

Old Tom settled his back against the tree and gazed at the sky. The clouds were passing quickly by. "Why," he replied, knowing it might take the lad years to puzzle out the answer — hard years but good years — "*Somewhen's* the best I know."

And then he closed his eyes and slept.

The Moon Child

There was once a land called Solin where all men worshipped the sun.

Children were born in the day and brought up in the sun's light. Lads and lasses courted at noon when the sun's power was at its height. And the dead were buried at the sun's waning and were afterward known only as shades.

All the people in Solin closed their doors when darkness fell. They gathered around their own home-fires for food and for prayer. There they sang hymns to the "little sun," as they called the flames that flickered in every hearth.

Now in that kingdom was a great forest which all men feared, for it was dense and dark and so tangled with undergrowth and so arched over with trees that no one dared enter it. The Solinians called it Swartwood, and they named it only in whispers.

Year by year the trees of Swartwood tried to advance on the kingdom. And year by year the men of

Solin cut the outermost trees back. It was these cut trees that burned in every hearth as a tribute to the sun.

Now it happened once in that kingdom that a baby was born, not at noon as was the custom, but at night in the light of the moon. Pale and wan, she grew tired in the sun and seemed to flourish only in the evening. And because of this, she was known as Mona, which meant "Moon Child."

Mona was a lonely girl, for her paleness frightened the other Solinians. They were all tanned and strong from the sun, while she seemed weakened by each day's light. They warned their children to leave her alone, and so the children did. For strangeness begets fear. Even Mona's own parents seemed to shun her, seeking out their own friends to walk with and work with in the sun.

So Mona learned to play by herself, seeking out the few shady places in Solin. And on the day she turned thirteen, forsaken by the children of her own age, she discovered the darkling woods.

Swartwood was a name used to frighten bad children. It was a place to make the strongest men in Solin tremble. But, to Mona, Swartwood was cool and inviting.

At first she had merely strolled by its edge, testing her fear of the stories told about the wood against her desire to know what lay hidden in its shade. And then,

on her birthday, the thirteenth one she had cele-
brated all by herself, she resolved to enter the dark
woods. If some evil befell her there, she thought it
would just serve to show her parents and neighbors
what her loss would mean to them.

She drew in a hasty breath, closed her eyes, and
walked down an arched-over path into the very heart
of the wood.

Nothing happened but the whisper of wind in her
ears and the cool shadows on her face. Mona opened
her eyes and looked around wonderingly.

There were soft mosses underfoot and climbing
flowers that bloomed when the sun started down.
There were ferns with fleshy leaves and fruit like
faded grapes. And on the bank of a transparent pool,
Mona discovered a large plant with brilliant purple
flowers and pods that were as clear as the water
nearby. At evening, refreshed and cooled, Mona returned to her home. No one, in fact, had missed her,
and where she had been she did not tell.

Soon Mona was slipping away from her house early
every morning and running into the woods when she
thought no one watched. She gave each plant a
name.

"This one," she said, pointing to a fragrant white
blossom, "shall be Moonflower. And this one Moon-
seed," she said, pointing to a climbing vine with
heart-shaped leaves. "And that fern I shall call

Moonwort." For the idea of the Moon would not leave her.

Mona built a bower of trailing vines and lined a path to the door with milky white rocks she called Moonstones. And for the first time in her life, Mona was content.

It was not long before the other children noticed that Mona was wandering down to the overshadowed paths. And after a while, the bravest of them followed her. By ones and by twos and by threes they crept to the edge of the forest to watch for her, though they did not dare go into the woods. Some called her names and some mocked her, but they waited a long time to see if she would return.

Return she did, in the late afternoon just before dusk, with a strange, contented smile.

The first day, the children who had waited laughed at her, and teased her with questions about the dark wood. Mona merely smiled. She pressed on them some of the cool white milky stones she had gathered from the woods. But they did not dare to take the stones and ran from her in fright.

The next day when Mona returned from the forest, the children taunted her and called her names. Again she said nothing but smiled and offered them fragile blossoms such as they had never seen before. And though many of the children ran away, a few of the girls thought the blossoms pretty and put them in their hair, where they seemed to grow and open with the coming night.

The third day all the children waited at the forest line. This time, when Mona appeared they questioned her again, and now, although they were still frightened they were also eager. And this time Mona answered them, the smile still playing on her mouth.

"There is a place," she said, "deep in the wood where it is neither night nor day, where sunlight and shadows meet and dance together in ever-changing ways."

The children repeated this to themselves, over and over and over again, until it became a chant. And they accepted her presents and brought them home.

But such angry scenes greeted them there. Fathers and mothers gathered the stones and blossoms and, in a crowd, marched to the edge of the darkling woods. There they threw the moon gifts as far as they could into the deepening shade.

"Lie there, devil rocks," they cried as the milky white stones went flying. "Grow there, devil seeds," they called as the fragile blossoms were caught by the wind.

The children did not understand their anger and were saddened by the loss of the gifts.

But the mothers and fathers of Solin could not throw away Mona's tale of the secret place in the wood or the impression her strange smile had made.

So the men of Solin gathered in angry councils, for fear begets anger. They argued before the safe bright hearthfires, first in one home and then the other. "She will bring the evil spell of Swartwood to our homes," they declared.

Their woodpiles grew taller than before as they cut back even more trees from the forest. But still it did not seem enough to make them feel safe.

"Her heart is as dark as the woods," they decided. And it was then that the people of Solin knew that Mona must be driven from their land, for anger seeks a victim.

So the men met and armed themselves. Their women formed behind them in a thin row. And behind them were the children, in scattered bunches, some weeping and some crying out, and all very much afraid. Only Mona's mother and father remained at home. They were mourning that such a thing had come to pass, though at the same time they were secretly relieved to be rid of her.

And late that afternoon, when the sun's shadows were beginning to lengthen on the land and Mona came out of the woods, she was met not by ones and by twos and by threes of curious children but by an angry mob of Solinians. They shouted and shook their fists and ran toward her, their raised axes gleaming dully in the sun.

The pale girl looked at them for a long moment, and then quickly turned and ran, ran back to the tree-arched, shadowy wood.

The people of Solin were, by that time, so angry that they chased right after her, waving their axes and fists at her back. They threw rocks and called out and hooted and made so much noise that before they realized it, they had run right into the woods.

But when the first trees had blotted out the sun, the men in the first rank grew frightened and stopped short. And the running women and children behind them bumped into them. The townspeople were shaken. They looked about uneasily at the trees above them and at the way the shadows crawled across their bodies.

Then the darkness was too much. With a single shout, the men and women turned around and ran back the way they had come. After a quick glance around, the children ran after them.

The little suns—the fires that burned that night in all the hearths of the village—seemed brighter and warmer than they ever had before.

Mona never returned. Fearing the axes and fists, she stayed and lived in her bower for the rest of her life. She learned which ferns made a balm and which made a meal. She fished in deep pools and farmed in small meadows. And if occasionally she missed the powerful sun or the bright sunflowers or the laughter of others, she did not say.

But strange—or was it?—one day years later, when she was old past fearing the axes and fists, she heard human voices in the forest. Some she almost recognized, for they were the other children, grown old as she. They came tentatively into the woods, by ones and by twos and by threes.

As they walked they talked of her, of Mona the pale girl, the child of the moon. And they saw the Moonstones, and the Moonflowers and Moonwort growing wild by the path. But though they searched for Mona in the green glades and in the hidden meadows, and they looked for her in the coppice, they never really found her where she waited, further out, always further out, in the place past the darkness where the sunlight and shadows met and danced together in ever-changing ways.

About the Author

Jane Yolen is known especially for her rare ability to create modern stories in the vein of the great classic folktales. Her poetic prose has won her many awards and honors. Born in New York, she is a graduate of Smith College. She worked for a time as an editor of children's books before she decided to become a full-time writer. She is married and lives with her husband and their three small children in a lovely old house in Hatfield, Massachusetts. Among her many distinguished books are *The Girl Who Cried Flowers,* winner of the 1974 Golden Kite Award of the Society of Children's Book Writers, Finalist for the National Book Award, and an A.L.A. Notable Children's Book; and *The Transfigured Hart,* an Honor Book for the 1975 Golden Kite Award.

About the Illustrator

David Palladini was born in Italy, but came to the United States when he was very young and grew up in Highland Park, Illinois. He received his art training at Pratt Institute in Brooklyn. In addition to illustrating books, Mr. Palladini has received many awards and citations for his work in poster design and the graphic arts. Jane Yolen's *The Girl Who Cried Flowers,* which he illustrated, was chosen by the *New York Times* for its list of The Best Illustrated Books of 1974, and was selected by the American Institute of Graphic Arts for the Bratislava International Biennale (B.I.B.) 1975.